USBORNE HOTSHOTS

CHESS

Edited by Rebecca Treays
Designed by Heather Blackham

Illustrated by Norman Young and Ian Winter
Photographs by Howard Allman and
Jane Munroe Photography

Series editor: Judy Tatchell
Series designer: Ruth Russell

Consultant: Clive Felton

CONTENTS

Starting off

Chess is a battle between two armies called Black and White. To play chess all you need is a chess set, made up of a chess board and the chess pieces (the two armies). There are 16 pieces in each army, but only six different kinds of pieces altogether. Each kind of piece has its own shape and its own way of moving on the board.

Pawn

Rook

Bishop

The photograph below shows the pieces set out at the beginning of a game.

Knight

Queen

King

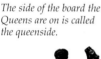
The side of the board the Queens are on is called the queenside.

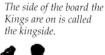
The side of the board the Kings are on is called the kingside.

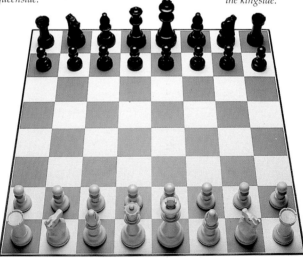

Although the pieces and the squares are always called Black and White, they don't actually have to be black and white as long as one is light and the other dark.

Following diagrams

In this book, most of the examples of chess moves are shown on diagrams like the one on the right. The chess pieces are represented as symbols and different sorts of moves are shown using different sorts of arrows and circles. You can find out about these below.

Diagram symbols

King   Queen

Rook   Bishop

Knight   Pawn

Shows a move

Shows a capture, with a circle around the captured piece

Shows an attack

Shows a potential move

How to play

Each player takes a turn to move one piece. White always starts, so change armies if you play a second game.

The winner of a game of chess is the person who can trap the enemy King. This is called checkmate.

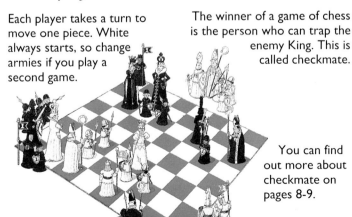

You can find out more about checkmate on pages 8-9.

The Queen

The Queen is your most powerful piece. She can move in any one direction for any number of squares. But she cannot jump over other pieces. If there is an enemy piece in the way the Queen can capture it. Find out about capturing below.

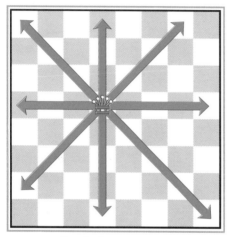

How the Queen moves.

At the start of the game, the Black Queen must always be on a black square and the White Queen must always be on a white square.

Each army only has one Queen so you must make sure you don't lose her early on in the game.

Capturing

Capturing an enemy piece weakens its army, making it easier for you to attack its King. To capture an enemy piece you have to land on its square with one of your own pieces. The captured piece is then removed from the board.

Here the Black Queen is capturing a White Bishop.

Pawns

Each player has eight Pawns at the start of the game. The word "pawn" comes from a Latin word meaning "foot-soldier". Your Pawns begin the game in the row in front of your other pieces.

How Pawns move.

The Pawns are usually the smallest pieces on the board.

Pawns normally move forward in a straight line, one square at a time. A Pawn's first move is special, though. For this turn only, you can choose whether to move it one or two squares forward.

Diagonal capture

A Pawn is the only piece that moves differently when it is capturing. Instead of moving straight ahead, it moves one square diagonally ahead. It cannot capture the piece directly in front of it.

Here a Black Pawn is capturing a White Bishop.

Promoting pawns

At the start of the game a Pawn is your least valuable piece. But, if a pawn reaches the other side of the board it can be exchanged for a Queen (or any other piece you like except for the King). You can do this even if your Queen is still on the board.

5

Bishops, Knights and Rooks

Bishops

Each player has two Bishops. Bishops move diagonally in any direction. They can move any number of squares each turn, but cannot jump over pieces in their way.

One Bishop moves diagonally on the black squares and the other on the white squares. This means a Bishop can only capture pieces on the same kind of square as itself.

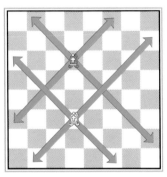

How Bishops move.

This Bishop cannot capture either of these White Pawns.

Knights

Each player has two Knights. The Knight is the only piece that can jump over other pieces. Knights move three squares at a time: two in one direction, then one to the side.

The Knights usually look like horses.

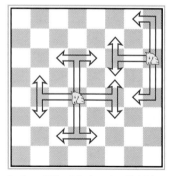

In the middle of the board, a Knight can attack eight squares but at the edge it can attack only four. So try to keep your Knights in the middle.

Rooks

There are two Rooks in each army. They start the game in the corners of the board. Apart from your Queen, Rooks are your most valuable pieces.

Rooks are sometimes called Castles.

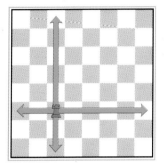

How Rooks move

Rooks can move as many squares as they like in straight lines, either to the front, to the back or to the sides. They cannot move diagonally.

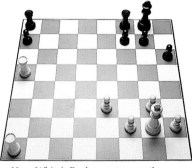

Here, White's Rooks are stronger than Black's, which are blocked in by Pawns.

Rooks work best on open lines (lines which are not blocked by other pieces) so they are most useful later in the game when there are fewer pieces on the board.

Jumping

Knights are especially useful at the beginning of the game.

This is because they can jump into the middle of the board even when there are Pawns in front of them.

Knights jumping into the middle.

Knights can often jump out of danger when being attacked by enemy pieces.

The King, check and checkmate

Your King is the most important piece in your army. He can never be taken off the board, but if he is trapped and cannot escape you lose the game.

The Kings are usually the tallest pieces.

The King can move in any direction but only one square at a time.

How the King moves.

Check

If an enemy piece is in a position from where it could capture your King, you are in check. The enemy piece is called the checking piece.

You must save your King from check right away. There are three ways of doing this.

1. Move the King out of the way of the enemy piece.

2. Move another piece in front of the King, so the King is out of the firing line.

3. Capture the checking piece, to remove the threat.

On the board on the left, the White Rook is putting the Black King in check. Black can escape by blocking the White Rook's path with his Queen, Knight or Bishop.

8

Checkmate

If you cannot save your King from check, this is called checkmate and you have lost the game. This happens if there are no squares to escape to, no pieces to block the attack, and no pieces that can capture the checking piece.

Teamwork

No chess piece, not even the powerful Queen, can give checkmate on its own. It always takes at least two pieces, and often more. So you must make your pieces work together as a team, defending each other and attacking the enemy King.

The Black Rook is moving to put the White King in check. White cannot save the King, so it is checkmate.

On this board, the White Queen gives checkmate, but only with the help of the Bishop, which defends the Queen.

Check etiquette

If you put your opponent's King into check, you say "Check" when you have finished your move.

It is against the rules to move your King onto a square where he will be in check. If you do, you must take your turn again.

Notation

The code for writing down chess moves is called notation. There are two main systems of notation: algebraic notation and descriptive notation.

This book uses algebraic notation. Once you can read notation, you can try out games written in magazines or books, using your own chess set.

The board

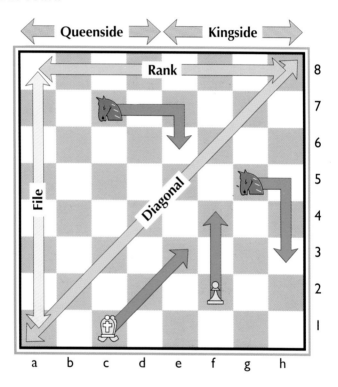

The board is divided into ranks, files and diagonals. Ranks are the rows of squares which run across the board. Files are the columns of squares which run up and down the board.

Diagonals run at a slant across the board. Each file is given a small letter and each rank is given a number. Each square is called by its file letter and its rank number.

The pieces

Each piece, except for the Pawn, is coded by a capital letter. The Pawn has no code letter.

Pawn has no code *Rook is R* *Knight is N*

Bishop is B *Queen is Q* *King is K*

The moves

To write down a move, first put the code letter for the piece. Then write the letter and number of the square it moves to. For a Pawn, just write the letter and number of the square it moves to. If a game is being recorded the moves are numbered. As White starts the game, White's moves are always written first.

Some moves may be possible for more than one piece. In order to identify which piece moves, the rank or file that it is on is written too.

Captures

When a piece captures, you write "x" between the code for the piece and the move it makes.

This move is Bxh8.

Check and checkmate

If a move gives check, "+" is written after the move.

If a move gives checkmate, "++" is written.

This move is Qxd8+.

The move on the right is Rxe8++.

11

Exchanges

Sometimes you cannot capture an enemy piece without losing one of your own. This is called an exchange. You should only exchange if the piece you lose is of the same, or less value, than the piece you capture. To help you decide if an exchange is worth it, the pieces are given points.

Pawn = 1 point   *Knight = 3 points*

Bishop = 3 points   *Rook = 5 points*

Queen = 9 points   *King = 0 points*

The King has no points because he can never be captured.

A fair exchange

It is a fair exchange to capture a piece that is of the same value as the one you lose.

Here, Black takes a Bishop (3) and loses a Knight (3).

A good exchange

It is a good exchange to capture a piece which is more valuable than the one you lose.

Black's Bishop (3) has captured White's Queen (9) and is then captured by a Pawn.

A bad exchange

It is a bad exchange to lose a piece that is more valuable than the one you capture.

White's Queen (9) has captured Black's Rook (5), only to be captured herself by the Black Knight.

Attacking and defending

On the board on the right, the White Rook moves to a position from where it can attack Black's Bishop. Black has two options. He can move the Bishop onto a safe square out of the Rook's line of attack. Or he can move the Knight so it could capture the Rook if it were to capture the Bishop. Only defend a piece in this second way if your opponent is going to lose a more valuable piece than yourself.

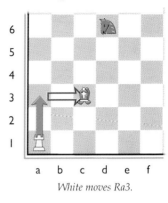

White moves Ra3.

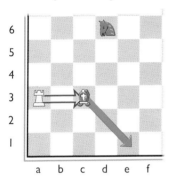

1. Black moves Be1, onto a safe square, out of the Rook's way.

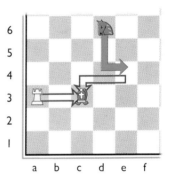

2. Black moves Ne4, so the Knight can take the Rook if it captures his Bishop.

Look first!

Always look carefully before you make any move. The square you move to may be guarded. On this board, the White Knight is moving to attack the Black Rook, but the square it moves to is defended by Black's Bishop. White will lose his Knight without gaining anything himself.

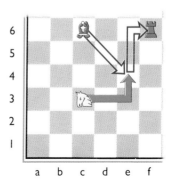

Castling and en passant

Castling

Castling is a special move for the King and the Rook. It helps to keep the King safe in the early part of the game, and brings the Rook nearer to the middle of the board where it is in a good position to attack.

Castling, shown below, is the only time you can move two pieces in one turn, and the only time you can move the King two squares at once.

To castle on the kingside, move the King two squares in the direction of the Rook. Move the Rook two squares the other way.

To castle on the queenside, move the King two squares in the direction of the Rook. Move the Rook three squares the other way.

Castling rules

1. It must be the first move of the game for both pieces.

2. There must be no pieces between the King and Rook.

3. The King must not be in check, either before castling or on the square where he ends up.

4. The King must not be in check on any of the squares he passes over during the move.

In notation, castling on the kingside is written as 0-0. Castling on the queenside is written as 0-0-0.

14

In this game, both Black and White have castled, so both armies have protected their Kings.

Here, neither side can castle. Black's King is in check from White's Knight. White has already moved his King.

Here, White has castled, but Black cannot, as the Black King would be in check as he passed through square f8.

Here, neither side can castle. White's King would be in check as he passed through f1. Black has pieces in the way.

En passant

When a Pawn moves two squares forward as its first move, an enemy Pawn can capture it as if it had moved only one square. This is called *en passant* (pronounced "on passon") which is French for in passing.

White captures the Black Pawn as if it were on this square.

15

The opening

The first few moves you make at the beginning of a game are very important. This is your chance to get your pieces into the best positions for the struggle in the middle of the game. Remember that White always moves first.

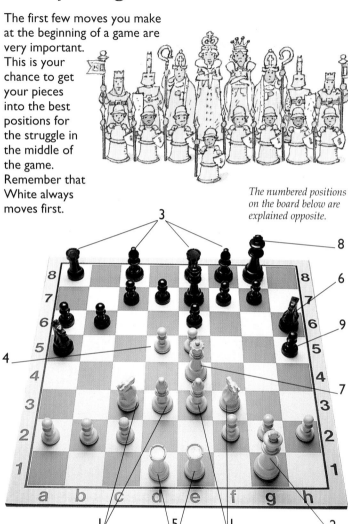

The numbered positions on the board below are explained opposite.

The most important thing at the beginning of the game is to move pieces to the middle of the board where they are most powerful. This is called developing. But remember that some pieces, such as Rooks, are stronger later in the game.

16

Key

1. Move Knights and Bishops into the middle of the board.

2. Castle early to keep the King safe.

3. Avoid blocking in your Bishops and Rooks.

4. Aim to control the middle of the board. Try to put Pawns on d4 and e4 or d5 and e5.

5. Place Rooks on those ranks and files least blocked by Pawns.

6. Keep Knights away from the edge of the board.

7. Position your Queen for attack – but not too early as she may be attacked.

8. Do not leave your King exposed to attack – avoid moving the Pawns in front of your King too early as this may leave your King vulnerable.

9. Do not waste time moving your side Pawns.

On the board opposite, White has made a good start but Black has made many mistakes. The key on the right explains the good and bad positions. You can use this as a guide when you play your own openings.

The middlegame

Once you have brought out most of your pieces, you begin the middlegame. This is the time when you should start trying to capture enemy pieces in order to weaken your opponent's position. Here are some special tricks you can use to attack your opponent's pieces.

A fork

A fork is an attack by one piece on two enemy pieces at the same time.

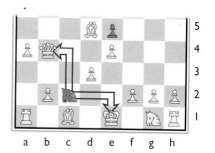

Here the Black Knight is attacking both the White King and Queen. White must move his King out of check, and so lose his Queen.

A skewer

A skewer is an attack on a valuable piece, forcing it to move so a less valuable piece is captured.

Here the Black Queen is being attacked by the White Bishop. The Queen has to move, leaving the Black Rook open to capture.

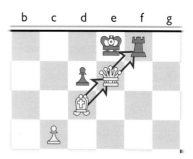

A pin

A pin is an attack on an enemy piece which is covering a more valuable piece.

Here the White Bishop has the Black Knight pinned to the Black Queen. The Knight cannot escape the Bishop's attack without losing the Black Queen.

Discovered attack

Another trick is the discovered attack. This happens when you move one piece to open the way for another of your pieces to attack an enemy piece. Watch out for discovered attacks on your own pieces.

By playing Bc7, White reveals a discovered check (a discovered attack which gives check), and attacks the Black Queen at the same time.

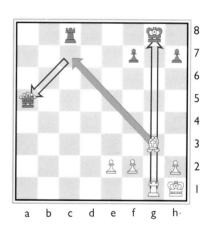

Questions to ask before your move

1. What is my opponent planning to do?
2. Are all my pieces defended? Are any being attacked?
3. How well is my King defended?
4. Can I capture an enemy piece? Is it safe to do so?
5. Are all my pieces working together as a team?
6. Are any of my pieces blocking my own advance?

Draws and other endings

Sometimes it is not possible for either side to checkmate the other and the game ends in a draw. There are two main types of draw: stalemate and perpetual check.

Stalemate

Stalemate happens when a player is not in check, but cannot make any move that is allowed. On this board, it is Black's turn to move but if he moves he will be in check from the White King or Queen. The King is not allowed to move into check so the game must end in stalemate.

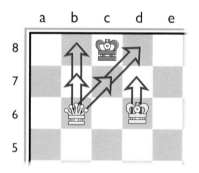

Perpetual check

In perpetual check, one player continually puts the other in check, but cannot get checkmate. If check is repeated three times, the game ends in a draw.

Here, the White King is in check from the Black Queen. The White King moves out of check to g1.

Black moves Qe1+. White moves Kh2. Black moves Qh4+ and the King has to move back to g1. The game is drawn.

Resigning

Apart from draws and checkmate, a game of chess can also end with one player resigning – so giving victory to his opponent. Some players do this when they feel their position is so hopeless, they have no chance of a win.

A player may show he has resigned by tipping over his own King. It is never a good idea to resign however, as your opponent may make a mistake which would allow you to draw or even win.

Players can also agree to draw, if neither side thinks that they can win.

The endgame

If neither player manages to give checkmate in the
middlegame, both sides gradually lose most of their
pieces. So then each side has to try to checkmate their
opponent with only a King and one or two other pieces.
This stage of a game is known as the endgame.

A typical endgame.

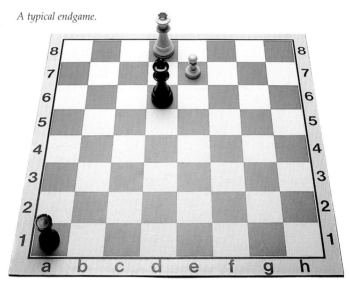

With some combinations of pieces, though, it is impossible to
give checkmate, even if your opponent only has a King left.

Can checkmate

👑 + ♛ against 👑

👑 + ♜ against 👑

👑 + ♝ + ♝ against 👑

👑 + ♝ + ♞ against 👑

👑 + ♛ against 👑 + ♜

Can't checkmate

👑 + ♝ against 👑

👑 + ♞ + ♞ against 👑

(unless the enemy King is in a corner)

👑 + ♞ against 👑

👑 + ♟ against 👑

(unless the Pawn can be promoted)

Hints for the endgame

1. If you have any Pawns left, concentrate on getting one of them to the other side of the board, so you can make it a Queen.

2. Try to keep all your pieces on open lines near the middle of the board, where they are most powerful. Now that you have very few pieces left make sure they are all working as a team.

3. Now is the time to bring out your King and to use it as an attacking piece.

Rooks endgames

In a Rook endgame each player has only a Rook, a few Pawns and the King. This is the most common type of endgame. On this board, both armies have pieces in exactly the same positions, except for their Rooks. This makes all the difference to the game. See how White's Rook gives it the advantage.

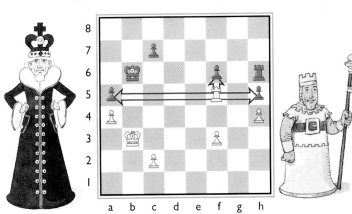

White's Rook is superbly placed, attacking Black's Pawns on a5, f6, and h5.

Black's Rook is trapped. It has to defend the Pawns on f6 and h5, and if it moves one of these Pawns will be lost.

The Black King must also stay on its square to defend the Pawn on a5.

White's Rook dominates the board. It controls Black's moves and gives the White King total freedom.

Pawns in the endgame

If you have any Pawns left in the endgame, they can be very valuable as one of them might be promoted to a Queen. This could give you a big advantage over your opponent, so move your Pawns carefully.

Blocking

Try to avoid blocking your Pawn with one of your own pieces, as has happened to Black on this board on the right.

Promoting in the endgame

In the game shown in the two boards below, both armies have the same number of pieces left. But only Black has a strategy for promoting a Pawn.

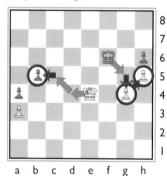

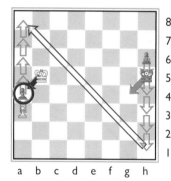

Black can promote as follows:
1. Kd4, Kg5; 2. Kc5, Kxg4; 3. Kxb5,
Kxh5; 4. Kxa4, Kg4.
Black's Pawn can now march up the
h-file to become a Queen.

White is unable to promote the Pawn on the a-file because, although it is unblocked, by the time it reaches a8, that square will be covered by Black's new Queen.

24

Use your other pieces to help your Pawn become a Queen. On this board, the White King is defending all the squares needed by the White Pawn to reach the other side.

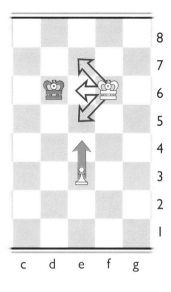

Decoys

A Pawn that is about to be promoted can be used as a decoy. While your opponent is trying to stop it, you can capture the pieces that are left undefended.

Here, Black moves Re8 to stop White promoting a Pawn. This leaves the Pawns on f5 and h5 unprotected. White then abandons the promotion plan and captures Black's Pawns.

Checkmate in the endgame

When you only have a few pieces left it is very difficult to checkmate the enemy King in the middle of the board. So it is vital that you force him into a corner, or at least to the edge of the board.

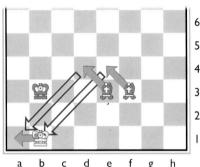

On this board, Black's two Bishops and King trap White's King.

Black moves 1. ... Be4+. White must then play 2. Ka1. Black's next move 2. ... Bd4, is checkmate.*

Here the Black King, Bishop and Knight can win, but it is more tricky. Black can only get checkmate if the enemy King can be forced onto a black corner square since the Bishop is on a black square. (If the Bishop is on a white square, the King must also be forced onto a white square.)

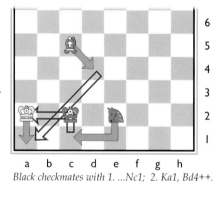

Black checkmates with 1. ...Nc1; 2. Ka1, Bd4++.

* Dots after the move number, for example **1. ... Be4+**, show a Black move without a White move. A White move alone is written without dots, for example **2. Ka1**.

26

If both sides have only a King and one other piece it is important to try to separate the enemy's pieces.

On this board, Black succeeds in separating White's Knight from the King, and so achieves checkmate.

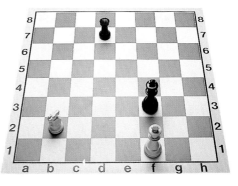

Black moves 1...Rd2 forcing the Knight to move to c4 or a4 to avoid capture. Black can then play 2...Rd1++.

Draws in the endgame

Here, Black has a King, a Bishop and a Pawn. But, surprisingly, this is not enough to win. White's King is positioned in a corner where he cannot be attacked by Black's Bishop.

Black will not be able to promote the Pawn as the White King is blocking the way. The game is most likely to end in stalemate, with for example: 1. Kg1, Bd4+; 2. Kh1, h2 stalemate.

Puzzles

Working on puzzles will help you to improve your chess skills.
You will find the answers to these eight puzzles on pages 30-31.

Pawn puzzle

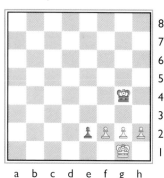

1. Black has one Pawn and White has three, but Black's Pawn is more powerful. Can you see why?

Knight puzzle

2. Can you spot a move for the White Knight that will allow White to win an important piece next move?

Bishop puzzle

3. Here, White's Bishops have driven the Black King into a corner. Find a move that gives White checkmate.

Rook puzzle

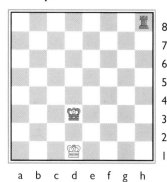

4. On this board, the Black King and Rook are about to checkmate the enemy King. Can you see how?

Queen puzzle

5. How many ways can the White Queen check the Black King and attack another piece at the same time?

King puzzle

6. The Black King has a brilliant move which will checkmate the White King. See if you can spot what it is.

Two-move mates

In these puzzles you have to think a little further ahead and find a sequence of two moves that leads to checkmate. After the first move and your opponent's reply, your second move should finish the game off by giving checkmate.

7. On this board, Black can checkmate the White King in the corner in just two moves. Black is to move next.

8. Black is in trouble at the end of this game. How can the White Knights be used to deliver checkmate? White to move.

29

Puzzle answers

1. Pawn puzzle Black can play **1. ... e1**, promote the Pawn to a Queen and checkmate the White King.

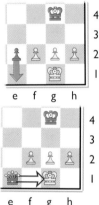

2. Knight puzzle White should play **Nb6+**. Black's only option is to play **Qxb6**. White can then capture Black's Queen with **cxb6**.

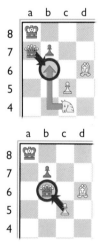

3. Bishop puzzle 1. Bb2++ traps the enemy King in the corner with no escape.

4. Rook puzzle 1. ... Rh1++

5. Queen puzzle The Queen has five checking moves shown on the board below. Each one leads to a capture.

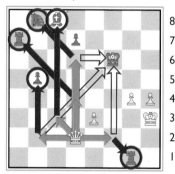

6. King puzzle 1. ... Kc7++. The White King is trapped in the corner and mated by a discovered check by the Bishop.

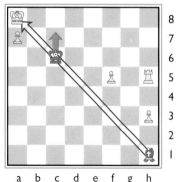

Two-move mates

7. 1. ... Nh3+ forces White to play **2. Kh1**. Black can then play **2. ... Bb7++**.

8. After **1. Ne7+**, Black can play only **1. ... Kh8**. Now White can play **2. Nfxg6++**. Black's Pawn on h7 cannot take the Knight as it is pinned to the King by the White Rook on h1.

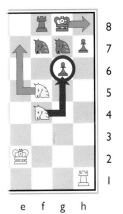

e   f   g   h

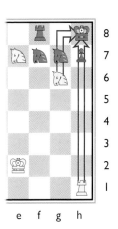

e   f   g   h

Useful addresses

UNITED STATES CHESS FEDERATION

186 Route 9 W
New Windsor
NY 12553
USA

THE CHESS FEDERATION OF CANADA

2212 Gladwin Crescent E-1
Ottawa
Ontario K1B 5N1
Canada

NEW ZEALAND CHESS FEDERATION

P.O. BOX 3130
Wellington
New Zealand

BRITISH CHESS FEDERATION

9A Grand Parade
St Leonard's on Sea
East Sussex
TN38 0DD
Great Britain

Chess words

Castling - A special move for the King and Rook. The King moves two squares toward the Rook and the Rook jumps over the King. (See page 14.)

Developing - Moving pieces early in the game to good squares in the middle of the board. (See page 16.)

Diagonal - A line of squares at a slant across the board.

Discovered attack - An attack that is only revealed when another piece moves out of the way. (See page 19.)

Endgame - The last part of the game when players have very few pieces left.

En passant - A special rule which allows a Pawn to capture an enemy Pawn that has moved two squares, as though it had moved only one. (See page 15.)

Exchange - Capturing an enemy piece, and in so doing losing one of your own pieces. (See page 12.)

File - A line of squares up and down the board.

Fork - An attack by one piece on two enemy pieces at the same time. (See page 18.)

Kingside - The side of the board on which the Kings start the game.

Middlegame - The stage of the game after the opening and before the endgame, when most pieces are captured and exchanged.

Notation - The code for writing down chess moves. (See page 10.)

Perpetual check - A type of draw where one player puts the other repeatedly in check but cannot achieve checkmate. (See page 21.)

Pin - An attack on a piece which cannot move, because if it did, a more valuable piece would be captured. (See page 19.)

Promoting a pawn - Making a Pawn which has reached the other side of the board into a more valuable piece. (See page 5.)

Queenside - The side of the board on which the Queens start the game.

Rank - A line of squares running across the board.

Skewer - An attack on a valuable piece which, when it moves, exposes a less valuable piece to attack and capture. (See page 18.)

Stalemate - A type of draw which occurs when one player can make no legal move but is not in check. (See page 20.)

This book is based on material previously published in *The Usborne Book of Advanced Chess*, *The Usborne Book of Chess Puzzles* and *Starting Chess*.

First published in 1995 by Usborne Publishing Ltd, Usborne House, 83-85 Saffron Hill, London EC1N 8RT, England.

Copyright © Usborne Publishing Ltd 1990, 1991, 1992, 1995

First published in America March 1996. UE

The name Usborne and the device are Trade Marks of Usborne Publishing Ltd. All rights reserved. No part of this publication may be reproduced, stored in a retrieval system or transmitted in any form or by any means, electronic, mechanical, photocopying, recording or otherwise without the prior permission of the publisher.

Printed in Italy.